The Gumdrop Tree
A Christmas Story

Written by Zeata Ruff

Illustrated by Jim and Zeata Ruff

First Edition

ISBN: 978-1-937449-25-4

Published by:

YAV Publications
Asheville, North Carolina

YAV books may be purchased in bulk for educational, business, fund-raising, or sales promotional use. For information, contact Books@yav.com or phone toll-free 888-693-9365.

Visit our website: www.InterestingWriting.com

3 5 7 9 10 8 6 4 2

Assembled in the United States of America

Published 2014

This book is dedicated to
our grandchildren:
Kayla, Beau, Kirby, Madison, & Kaden

The beautiful ornaments in our life.

Susie and Michael could hardly wait. It is Christmas Eve and this is the morning they will go up into the mountains with their father and find the biggest, finest, prettiest Christmas tree ever! Each and every year, the three of them put on their boots and warmest clothes. Father gets his axe, Michael gets the sled, and they go high into the mountains where the best Christmas trees grow.

It is the same with every family in their small town. They all gather in the town square, laughing and singing Christmas carols. As they make their way up the mountain, each family brags that this year it is their turn to find the best tree.

"Hurry up, Michael," Susie yelled at her brother, as he pulled the sled up the mountain. "All of the good ones will be gone and we'll have to take a little 'ole skinny one!"

"Don't worry, Susie, there'll be plenty for everybody," Father told her.

"Yeah, I know. But this year I want a huge tree. One that reaches the ceiling in our house. One that's so fat we'll have to move all the furniture just to get it in the living room. This year I want the very best tree ever! The most special one of anybody!"

"You need to remember, little one, it's not the size of the tree that makes it special," Father answered. "It's the thought and love that's behind it."

"What do you mean, Father?" Susie asked, very puzzled.

Before she could get her answer, someone was yelling that they had found their tree.

3

"Look! Look at this one," Freddie called to his father. "This is just the one! The very best one. Let's get this one, father."

Freddie's father agreed and soon the tree was chopped down and on its way to their house.

And that's the way it went all morning. First Freddie has his tree, then the Millers found a big round one. Mary Alice's dad cut one down that almost reached the sky. Joey and Andy found one with a little bird's nest snuggled in the branches. But no matter how much Susie searched, she could not find just the right one.

All of the families had cut their trees and started dragging them down the mountain. All but Susie.

"We've got to choose one, Susie. By the time we get it cut and down the mountain, it is going to be almost dark. We still have to get it up and decorated tonight," her father pleaded as they looked over what seemed like the hundredth tree.

"But we have to find
just the right one, Father,
and it has to be perfect," she
answered as she slowly circled yet another
tree, looking it over carefully for any broken branches.

"This is it! Look! It's really tall. Taller than you are, Father,
and it's big and fat. This is the one."

"Yes, Susie, I think you are right," he answered, glad that his
daughter had finally chosen a tree.

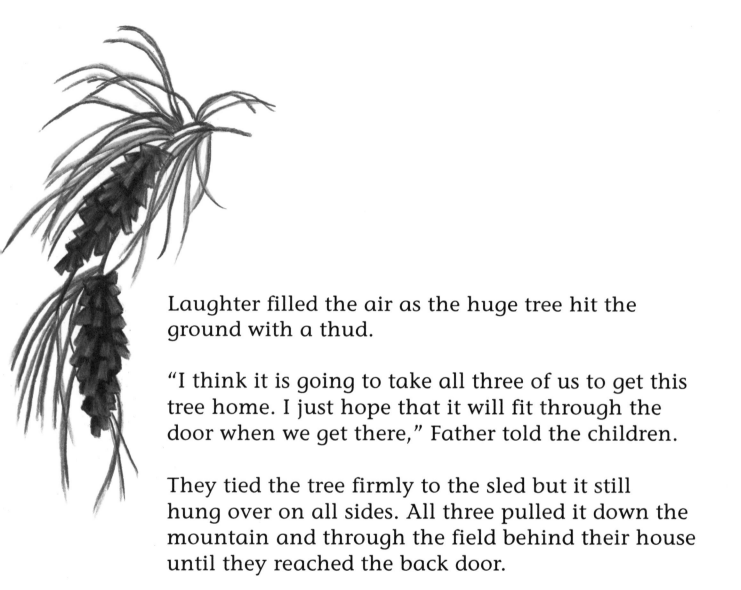

Laughter filled the air as the huge tree hit the ground with a thud.

"I think it is going to take all three of us to get this tree home. I just hope that it will fit through the door when we get there," Father told the children.

They tied the tree firmly to the sled but it still hung over on all sides. All three pulled it down the mountain and through the field behind their house until they reached the back door.

"What a wonderful tree!" Mother exclaimed as she stood on the back porch watching her husband cut off the few bottom branches so he could nail the stand on the trunk. "I do believe that this is the best tree that we've ever had. I know that it is the largest one."

"I found it, Mama," Susie bragged as she circled the tree one more time.

"I believe
that we have a tag-a-long,"
Father told them as he carefully
pulled a prickly little bush from the
branches of the fir tree. "A thorn bush
has gotten stuck to this side as we've pulled
the tree through the field." He tossed the small,
unwanted bush with its sharp thorns over the porch rail.

"Everybody grab hold and let's see if we can get this inside."

Father strung the lights, going up and down every limb until the tree glowed from the corner of the living room. Michael and Susie hung each of the colorful ornaments with care.

Standing on a chair on tip-toe, it was all Father could do to reach to the top and place the star.

Susie stepped back and admired the beautiful fir tree. Lights twinkled from every branch. Ornaments of every color glistened from each twig. It is the most wonderful tree ever, she though to herself.

"Come on, Susie, I need you to take supper over to Miss Martha before it gets too late," Mother called as she went into the kitchen. "I have it ready. Put your gloves and boots on because it's beginning to snow again."

"Oh, Mama, don't make me go. I don't like old Miss Martha. She's mean and grouchy and never smiles," Susie begged, still admiring her tree. "Let Michael take it."

"No, you have to go. Michael is helping your father," Mother told her as she placed the warm food in a basket and covered it with a cloth. "Now hurry up so it won't get cold. It's so late, I'm sure that Miss Martha thinks that we have forgotten her."

"But Mama, I don't like to go over there. She's old and she's mean." Susie pleaded again, not wanting to leave her beautiful tree.

"She's not mean, Susie. She's just lonely. Miss Martha has no family and it is difficult for her this time of the year. And yes, Susie, she is old and can't do as well as we can," Mother patiently explained. "So that means that it's our responsibility to help look after her and do what we can to try and make her life a little easier. Now hurry up. It's Christmas Eve and time all good children need to get into bed."

"Hold the basket carefully, Susie. Don't let it spill out," Mother told her, placing the basket of steaming food in her hands. "All you have to do is knock and when she comes to the door, take it inside and set it on her table."

"Oh, I almost forgot, here are some gumdrops. They are Miss Martha's favorite. I'll put the bag in your pocket but don't forget to give them to her."

As Susie carefully made her way down the steps, her mother called, "And be nice to her, Susie. Be sure to wish Miss Martha a Merry Christmas."

The snow was beginning to place a layer of white on everything. Glistening in the streetlights, it made even the smallest blade of grass twinkle. Thank goodness it's not far to her house, Susie thought. I'll just say "Here's your food and I hope you have a Merry Christmas," and get out of there.

The tall hedge that surrounded Miss Martha's yard looked dark and scary even with it's blanket of white.

Susie knocked once. No sound. She waited and then knocked again, louder. She could hear soft shuffling footsteps and the thump of a cane coming toward the door.

Miss Martha was tiny with stooped shoulders. Her white hair matched the snow outside. She was wrapped in a long black shawl that was constantly getting tangled in her cane. She opened the door so Susie could come inside.

"Mother sent you some soup and cornbread. Said you should eat it right away before it gets cold," Susie stated as she placed the basket on the old woman's table.

The room was dimly lit but it was easy to see that the small kitchen was very bare. There was no teapot singing on the stove or warm cookies waiting for someone to pick them up.

15

In the center of the small table was a straggly twig, probably broken off the hedge outside. It had two small balls of foil nestled between the leaves and the bottom was surrounded by a red scarf.

"What's that, Miss Martha?" Susie ventured to ask, pointing at the sagging branch.

"Why, that's my Christmas tree," she answered.

Not sure just what to think, Susie kept looking first at the strange tree and then at Miss Martha and back again.

"My mother says I should wish you a Merry Christmas," Susie said as she quickly began to make her way to the door. She still was not sure what to think of the strange tree.

"Where's your scarf, child?" the old woman asked the puzzled little girl. "It's beginning to snow hard and you'll catch a cold.

"Guess I forgot it," Susie told her, wanting to get out of the house as quickly as she could.

"Well, here take this one," Miss Martha said, taking the red scarf from around the bottom of her tree. She gently placed the bright material around Susie's neck and tied it snug under her chin. "Merry Christmas to you, too, child."

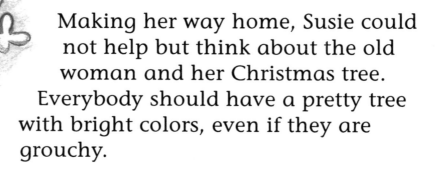

Making her way home, Susie could not help but think about the old woman and her Christmas tree. Everybody should have a pretty tree with bright colors, even if they are grouchy.

But how could she get Miss Martha a tree? It was already late and even if she could find one, she certainly didn't have any decorations for it.

It was beginning to snow harder as Susie started up her back steps. She saw the discarded branches that her father had cut from the bottom of their tree. Maybe she could tie them together. But even if it worked, she still had no decorations.

"Ouch!" The thorn bush had caught on her pants and scratched her leg. It took several minutes but she was finally able to free herself. Susie sat on the edge of the porch, not ready to go inside where everything was warm and inviting. Not wanting to admire her beautiful tree with its colorful decorations, she stared at the little thorn bush that was such a problem.

Shoving her cold hands into her coat pockets, she discovered the bag of gumdrops that she had forgotten. Her mother would be very displeased that she had not given the gift to Miss Martha.

There they were, with all their bright colors. The sugar coating made them glisten like ornaments on a tree. If only they were ornaments, Susie thought.

Then she had an idea!

Carefully picking up the thorn bush, she began placing the candy on each sharp point. Filling the tree with all the beautiful colors, it began to look like a miniature Christmas tree just like the one standing in her living room.

"Susie, is that you?" Mother called from the doorway. "It's too cold for you to be sitting out here. What are you doing anyway?" She asked as she stepped out onto the porch.

"I'm making Miss Martha a Christmas tree," Susie answered as she placed the last gumdrop on the bush. "I forgot to give her the candy, Mama, so I'm going to take it to her."

Away she ran before her mother could stop her. Holding the colorful little thorn bush high in the air, her feet barely touched the ground.

Finishing the last bit of soup and bread, Miss Martha was startled to hear the knock on her door. She opened it only a crack to peek outside and see who could be calling at this late hour.

"It's me, Miss Martha. It's me, Susie! I've brought you something. May I come in, please?"

The door opened wider and the two just stood there for a moment looking at each other.

"It's a Christmas tree, Miss Martha," Susie explained as she gently handed the strange gift to the old woman. "Not a real one. But one with bright colors and it's got your favorite candy on it, too."

The two carefully put the new tree on the table in the place of the scraggly hedge. Susie took the red scarf from her neck and wrapped it around the bottom of the new tree.

Stepping back, they both admired the small bush with its colorful ornaments.

"Merry Christmas, Miss Martha. Merry Christmas."

"Merry Christmas to you, too, child. This is the most beautiful Christmas tree I've ever had."
It was all she could say as a tear rolled down her cheek.

Now I know what Father meant, Susie thought on her way home. "It's not the size that makes a Christmas tree special, it's the thought and love behind it."